For Michael E., who believed in
me and never gave up.
G.R.

For Joanne, Emily, Holly and
Sarah... my stars.
M.R.

First published in 2007
by Meadowside Children's Books
185 Fleet Street, London, EC4A 2HS
www.meadowsidebooks.com

Text © Michael Rack 2007
Illustrations © Graham Ross 2007

The rights of Michael Rack to be identified as the author
and Graham Ross as the illustrator of this work have been
asserted by them in accordance with the Copyright, Designs
and Patents Act, 1988

A CIP catalogue record for this book is available
from the British Library
Printed in China

10 9 8 7 6 5 4 3 2 1

EDWARD BUILT A ROCKETSHIP

Michael Rack • illustrated by Graham Ross

meadowside
CHILDREN'S BOOKS

"I'll do a dance on Venus,
And have a snack on Mars.

Edward looked into the sky
And said "I think I might
Shoot across the galaxy
At ten o'clock tonight.

I'll read a book on Saturn
By the light of all the stars."

The more he looked, the more he thought, about his master plan,
"I need to get myself up there as quickly as I can!"

He put things here,

                he put things there,

So Edward built a rocket ship,
Designed to fly so far.
He built it from some odds and ends
And bits from Daddy's car.

And added loads of stuff.

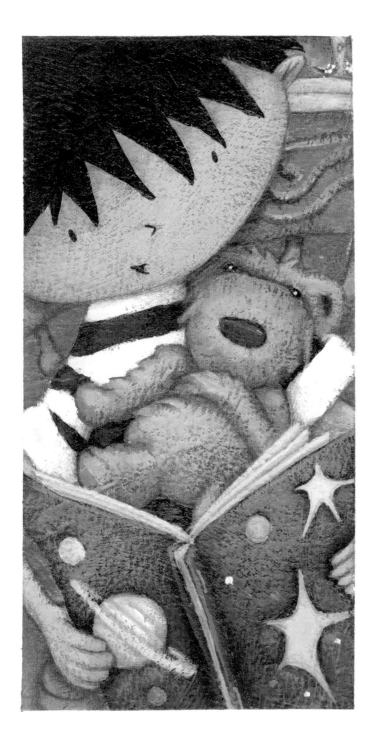

His mother kissed him on the nose
And handed him a snack.
    "Say hello to Mercury,
    But don't be too late back!"

He even packed his teddy bear,
    In case it got too rough.

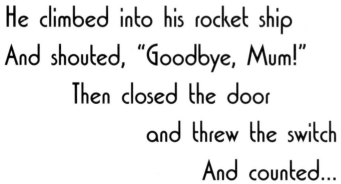

He climbed into his rocket ship
And shouted, "Goodbye, Mum!"
Then closed the door
and threw the switch
And counted...

...1

He closed his eyes...

and held on tight.

The engines went...

Then there he was, in deep blue space...

...heading for the moon.

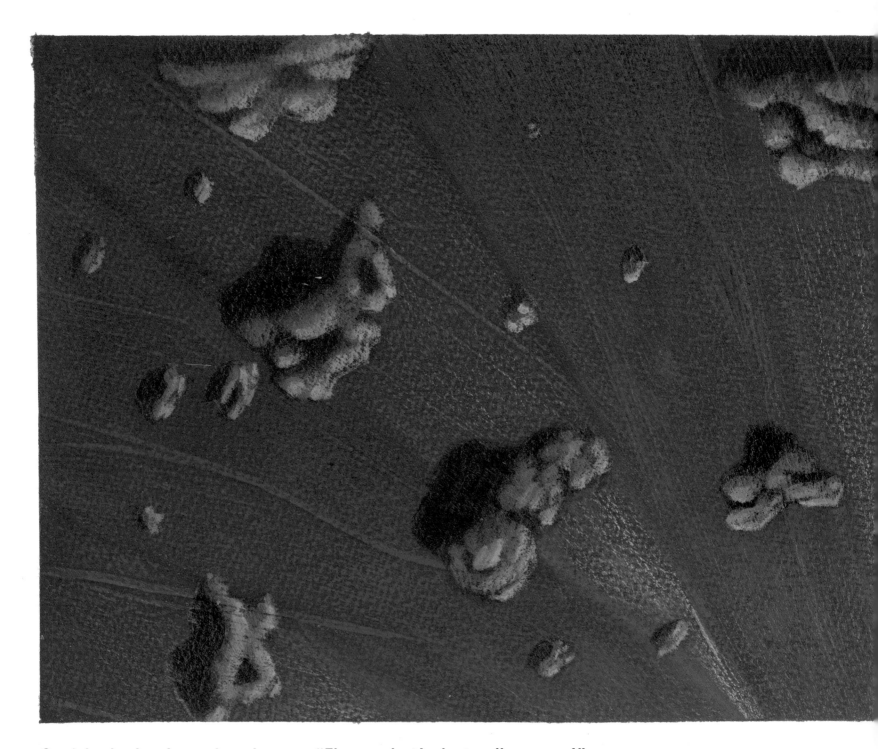

Suddenly he heard a bang. "The rocket's lost all power!"
He looked outside and thought, "Oh no! I'm in a meteor shower!"

A rock had hit his ship quite hard and left a nasty crack.
Edward told his teddy bear, "We might not make it back!"

Then Edward heard another noise. A giant UFO!

But when he looked, an alien waved and offered him a tow.

They took him for some quick repairs and fixed his broken ship

Then off he went to Jupiter, continuing his trip.

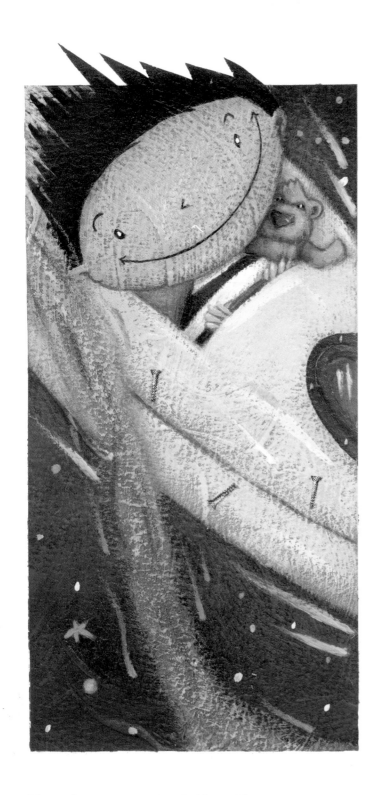

He drove around the Universe,
And chased an asteroid.

Saturn, Neptune, Uranus
Were planets he enjoyed.

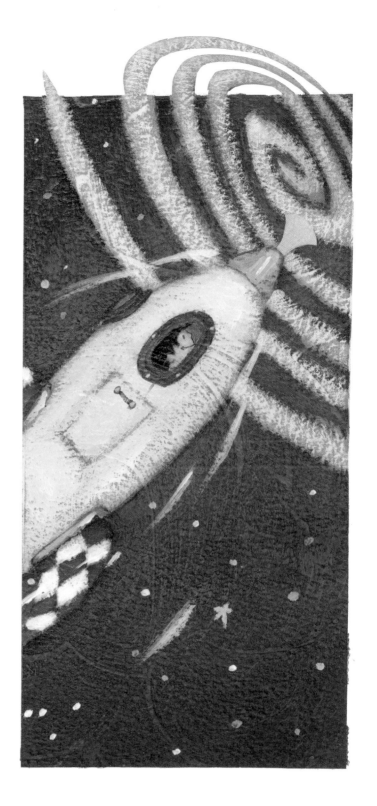

He waved at passing astronauts,
And steered past satellites.

He headed for the Milky Way
To look at all the sights.

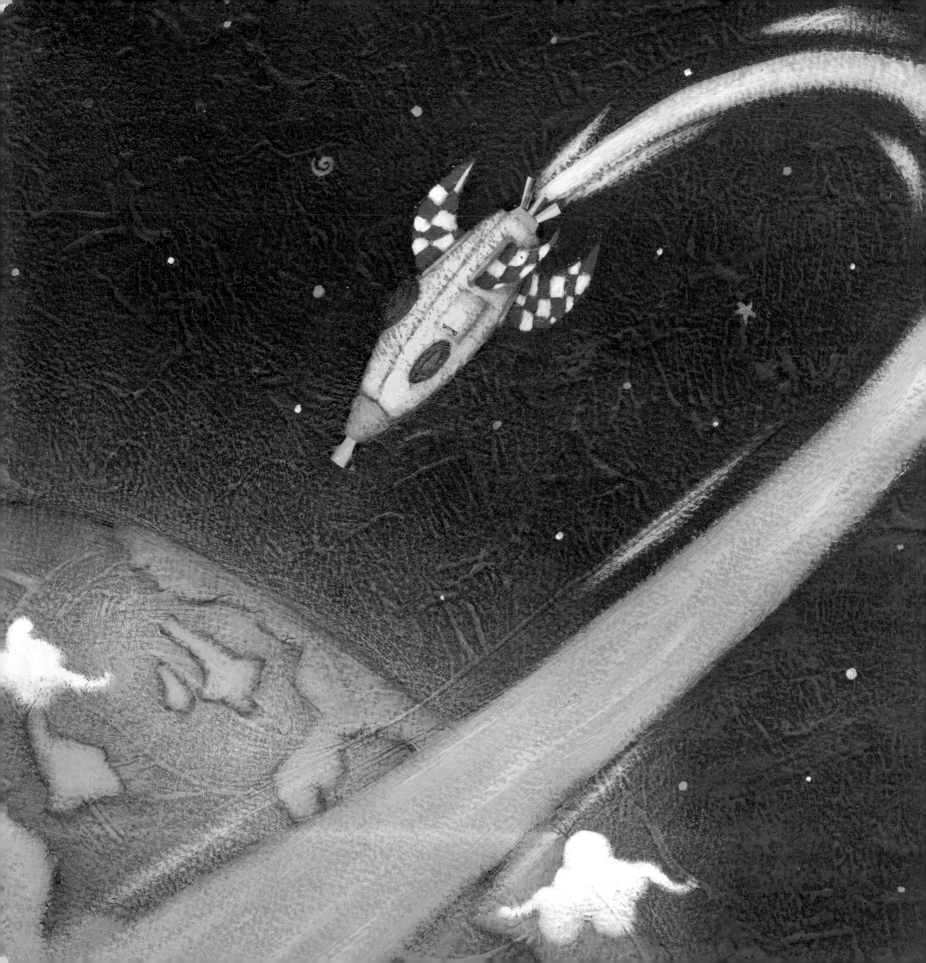

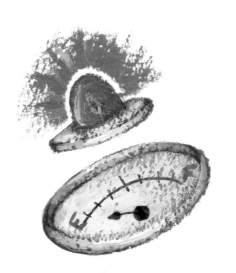

By now his fuel was getting low.
He saw the Earth's blue sea,
He turned around his ship and said,
"Now, that's the place for me!"

So, he and Teddy dropped to Earth,
Strapped tight into their seats.
He pulled a cord that launched a chute
He'd made from Mummy's sheets.

He floated down through fluffy clouds and rode in on the breeze.
Then finally he saw his house and landed in the trees.

He ran into his mother's arms and said, "I've touched the sky!
I've made a billion stars my friends...

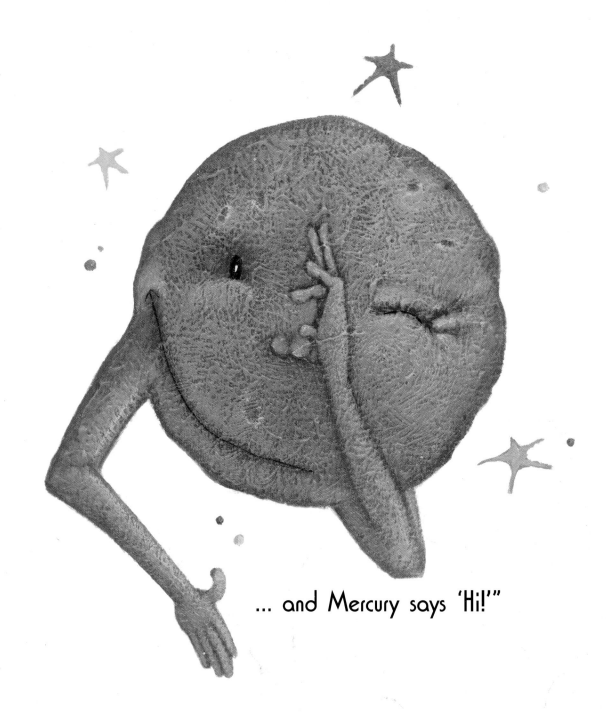

... and Mercury says 'Hi!'"